# KENT
# STATE

# KENT STATE

DEBORAH WILES

SCHOLASTIC PRESS

New York

Library of Congress Cataloging-in-Publication Data available

ISBN 978-1-338-35628-1

10 9 8 7 6 5 4 3 2 1     20 21 22 23 24

Printed in the U.S.A  23
First edition, April 2020

Book design by Elizabeth B. Parisi

For Allison, Jeff, Sandy, and Bill,
for the shepherds of their stories,
and for those who come next:
the innocents and the activists,
the questioners and the debaters,
the voters and the proclaimers,
the realists and the idealists,
the truth-seekers, the young

*"War. What is it good for?"*
—Edwin Starr

# prelude

America's troop involvement in the Vietnam War began in 1964 and ended in 1973. In those nine years, over 58,000 Americans died, most of them under the age of twenty-five. Nineteen- and twenty-year-olds serving in Vietnam were not yet old enough to vote at the start of the war but were old enough to die for their country more than 8,000 miles away from home.

By 1968, the number of American troops in Vietnam reached a peak of 543,482. Over 40,000 American service members had already died, and the war, which had been justified as a means to stop the worldwide spread of Communism by supporting South Vietnam in its stand against the Communist Viet Cong soldiers of the North (who were backed by Russia and China), now seemed unwinnable to a majority of the American people.

President Lyndon Baines Johnson put a troop drawdown into effect and chose not to run for reelection in 1968, instead spending the remainder of his time in office overseeing the effort to end the war through a negotiated peace with the Communist North Vietnamese.

Troop levels dropped to 475,200 in 1969 as Americans trained the South Vietnamese to fight their war against the Viet Cong, who refused to come to the negotiating table. President Richard Nixon asked Congress to institute a draft lottery system whereby young men who had previously had deferments that kept them from going to Vietnam if they were in college would be entered into the draft pool each year, determined by the number assigned to their birthdays.

Local draft boards across the country retained the right to decide exemption or deferment status based on a questionnaire all eighteen-year-old males had to fill out when they registered for the draft. All registrants were listed as 1-A—draft-ready—until or unless they received a deferment or an exemption. As the war waged on, and as draft boards had to meet their quotas for inductees, these deferments became more arbitrary, depending on how each draft board ruled on each registrant's application for deferment or exemption, and the rulings could change as well, which left all young men over eighteen, including those in college, uncertain about their future.

Nixon widened the war with carpet-bombing campaigns even as he continued troop withdrawal. On March 18, 1970, the U.S. began bombing neutral Cambodia, a country next door to Vietnam and a safe harbor for North Vietnamese troops.

This news became public on April 30, when Nixon appeared before the American people on television to announce the beginning of an "incursion" (not an "invasion") for the purposes of rooting out Communist North Vietnamese strongholds in Cambodia and protecting the remaining U.S. troops in Vietnam.

This strategy was met with strong and visceral disapproval by the American people, particularly by the young. Across the country, students on college campuses protested, loudly and boldly and angrily, exercising their constitutional, First Amendment rights of freedom of speech, assembly, press, and petition.

At Kent State University in Kent, Ohio, student protests were met with the Ohio National Guard's occupation of the campus and, on May 4, 1970, the murder of four Kent State students and the wounding of nine others when National Guard troops opened fire on demonstrating students as well as on some who were observing or walking to class.

This book chronicles those four days in May 1970 when America turned on its unarmed children, in their schoolyard, and killed them.

# lament

*"I ain't marching anymore."*
—Phil Ochs

You are new here,
and we don't want to scare you away,
but we want you to know the truth,
so we will start by telling you what is most important:

They did not have to die.

> *But they did die.*
> *They were sacrificial lambs,*
> *coldly, deliberately slaughtered.*

No, they weren't—it was a mistake.
A tragic mistake.

> *It was calculated!*
> *Planned!*
> *They were lambs!*

It was a tragic mistake.

> *You don't have the whole story.*

And you always think you do.

*I know what I saw. I know what they did. I know that those kids
will never wear tat sleeves or gauges or listen to Mötley Crüe or
watch Star Wars or read Harry Potter or talk on a cell phone
or use a computer or play video games or realize the Vietnam
War is over and their unwilling, unknowing, unplanned-for
sacrifice helped it come to an end.*

Yes. It's a tragedy.

*And now there are other wars! More wars.
War after war after war.*

War is never over.

*It's over if we want it to be.*

War is never over.

*John Lennon said it was. "War is over if you want it."
It's in a song he and Yoko wrote in 1971.
Too late for Allison, Bill, Sandy, and Jeff to hear it.*

Are we going to argue again?

*Yes. We always argue when we speak of the killings.*

Let's try not to argue.
Let's tell it the way we remember it, all of us.
Because, look, we have someone new here,
someone new to listen to us.

*I see that.*
*Hail, young friend . . . you are a feast for heartsick eyes.*
*I can tell, you are about the same age that Allison was.*
*Allison and her "flowers are better than bullets."*
*That's what she said to the National Guard soldiers,*
*the day before they killed her.*

I think our new friend looks like Bill. Bill was an Eagle Scout.

*Or Sandy—I loved Sandy.*
*She was wearing a red sweater that day.*

Or maybe Jeffrey. Jeffrey went to Woodstock!
And then, on May 4, 1970,
less than a year later,
he was shot through the mouth and killed
instantly.

*I loved Jeffrey so much. I loved them all.*

I did, too, of course.

*Nine were wounded. Don't forget them.*

I can't forget them.

*Or us.*
*We were all wounded that day.*

Yes. We all bear the scars of that day.
Our country bears the scars of that day.

*We are forever heartsick.*

Yes. So let's tell the story
one more time,
for our new friend.
Let's try not to argue.

*I can try not to argue, so long as you don't invite the others.*

The others will come.
They always come when we remember.
I tell them they are part of the story,
even when they disagree with me.

*\*I\* disagree with you.*

We won't be able to stop them from coming.
The ones who think those four deaths were justified.
The ones who think more kids should have been shot.
Killed.

*I hate them.*

There is no place for hate here.
Not anymore.

*I hate them.*

The ones who want us to forget—
they will come, too.

*The ones who tried to erase the fact that*

*grown-up America*
*killed its children in 1970*
*and never apologized for it.*

*I hate them.*

Tell the story, then.
This is a place for remembrance.
And for sharing what we remember
so it won't happen again.

*But it WILL happen again. It always happens again.*

It doesn't have to.
You start.
I promise not to argue until you've finished.
You start.

*I'll try.*
*But don't expect me to agree with you.*
*I don't even like you.*

You don't have to like me.
Just tell our new friend what you remember.

*I like it better when you tell it and I disagree.*

Then I will start.
Let me make room for our new friend.
We don't want to scare you away, friend.
Take the most comfortable chair.
Sit. Listen.

Make up your own mind.

Open your heart.

Here is what is most important:

They did not have to die.

# Friday
# May 1, 1970

*"What are we fightin' for?"*

—Country Joe McDonald

It was a beautiful day; that needs to be said—
the first beautiful spring day in Kent,
after a long, dark, cold Ohio winter—

*And Nixon!*

Yes, that speech.
Now we knew the war was going to go on.
And on.
We knew more would die.

*More would be us!*

More would be the innocent—

*Us!*

Yes, us, too. If our grades dropped,
we'd be drafted—

*You'd be drafted if your draft board*
*decided they needed to meet a quota!*
*It was totally arbitrary—no one was safe!*

Well, dropping out was a sure way
to get drafted!
So in addition to a degree in
English, or business, or physics,
we went to college and
majored in Avoiding the Draft.

*Did you get the flyer that morning?*
*About burying the Constitution?*

I got it.
Steve and Chris were handing them out
even before breakfast.

*President Nixon has flagrantly violated our constitutional*
*rights by invading a sovereign nation without a declaration*
*of war by Congress. Nixon has garnered all governmental*
*power to the executive and committed us to a course of*
*national barbarity; a crime that we will never be able to shed.*
*He has been motivated only by his own personal whims. He has*
*neither consulted Congress or the citizens of the United States.*
*In essence he has usurped power in a fashion not dissimilar to*
*a coup d'etat. President Nixon has murdered the Constitution*
*and made a mockery of his claim to represent law and order.*
*In recognition of the deceased we will commit the Constitution*
*to the earth at 12:00 noon today, on the Commons in front of the*
*Victory Bell.*

Did you memorize that?

*You bet I did.*

And you went to the burial.

> *You know I did. I'll never understand*
> *why you didn't.*
> *There was even an Army ROTC kid there*
> *who tried to stop us*
> *from burying a copy of the Constitution,*
> *but we booed him outta there.*
> *Then some kids tacked up a sign:*
> *WHY IS THE ROTC BUILDING STILL STANDING?*

Some of us were in class on Friday—
you know, keeping our grades up,
Avoiding the Draft—

> *That ROTC kid was going to*
> *end up in Vietnam for sure;*
> *he didn't need to worry about*
> *getting drafted—*
> *he'd signed up! Crazy!*

We heard a kid
burned his draft card
at the burial ceremony.

> *Yep.*
> *You could get arrested for that—*
> *Our "esteemed" U.S. Congress*
> *passed a law in 1965 against*
> *destroying or mutilating your draft card.*

That only made more kids do it.

And every guy over eighteen
had a draft card,
because we had to register for the draft
at eighteen.

*Jim Geary burned*
*his discharge papers!*
*He was awarded the Silver Star*
*in Vietnam, and now here he was,*
*a graduate student at Kent,*
*protesting*
*against the war that Friday,*
*at the burial of the Constitution*
*and the rally.*
*That was something.*

That would have been worth
missing class to see.

YOU *ALL* SHOULD HAVE BEEN
IN CLASS!
YOUR PARENTS SACRIFICED
TO GIVE YOU AN EDUCATION!
FIRST GENERATION
IN YOUR FAMILY TO
GO TO COLLEGE
AND *THIS*
IS HOW YOU
SHOW YOUR
THANKS?

*Here we go.*

it wasn't them, dear, it was the outside agitators.

the fbi called them radicals, remember?

said they were infiltrating college campuses,

those students for a democratic society, too.

You mean SDS.

we stand corrected. those sds'ers.

*It was us! Go away!*
You're *the outside agitators,*
*you townies!*

WE KNOW WHAT WE KNOW!
SDS'ERS! AND WEATHER FORECASTERS!

*hahahaha!*

Weathermen.

*The Weather Underground!*
*Get it right.*
*They were* really *radicals.*

THEY CAME TO YOUR CAMPUS!
THEY RECRUITED YOU TO THEIR CAUSE!
BERNADINE DOHRN!
SHE MET WITH THE VIET CONG!
MARK RUDD!
HE SHUT DOWN COLUMBIA UNIVERSITY!
YOU THINK WE DON'T KNOW THOSE NAMES
OR WHAT THEY DID?

WE SAW IT ON THE NEWS!
WE KNEW ALL ABOUT IT!

we were scared.

*Lots of people came to speak at Kent State—*
*that's what a college campus is for!*
*We were learning from (and becoming)*
*radicals, revolutionaries, thinkers—*

Not so different from our Ohio parents, really.
Union workers, labor organizers,
policy makers—

*Strikers—*

Yes, agitators who knew
how to strike and
bargain and
vote for change.
We grew up at their kitchen tables,
listening to them talk
about defending labor,
freedom, country,
dignity, and choice.

YOU ALL ARE NOTHING
BUT
COMMIE HIPPIE PINKOS!
YOUR PARENTS WERE
ASHAMED OF YOU!

*They were not!*
*We were patriots!*
*We had the right to assemble.*
*The right to protest.*
*Our parents taught us this.*
*They were auto workers,*
*meat cutters, pipe fitters,*
*truck drivers, teachers, nurses,*
*stay-at-home moms.*
*They taught us to love our country, too.*

                                  YOU NEVER SHOWED ANYTHING
                                          BUT CONTEMPT
                                      FOR OUR COUNTRY!
                                    YOU *HATE* OUR COUNTRY!

*OUR country hated US.*

Everyone calm down.
We each hold some of the truth.

        *We were* not *communists.*
        *We were* not *outside agitators.*
        *We were students. We belonged.*
        *It was our college. Our future.*

                                        BUT IT WAS OUR TOWN!
                                          YOU RUINED IT!
                                COMING INTO KENT WITH YOUR
                                      FAKE IDs,
                              GETTING DRUNK IN OUR BARS,
                                    BREAKING WINDOWS,

TRESPASSING,
SETTING FIRES IN THE STREET
BECAUSE YOU DIDN'T WANT TO
SUPPORT OUR PRESIDENT
AND HIS GOOD-FAITH ATTEMPTS
TO END THE WAR.

*Let me at them!*

Calm down. Stop.

it was so scary
when they started rocking our car
while we were stopped at the light downtown.
remember that?
it was may 1,
the night before the kentucky derby,
and we were on our way
to a party at the dixes'—
remember them?
they owned the newspaper, and
we had to get special permission
from the police
to stay out after eight because of
the curfew.

*Ha! The curfew was retroactive*
*on Friday night!*
*Get your facts straight!*

You can't make a curfew retroactive.

*That's what they did, though.*
*Suddenly there was a curfew*
*nobody knew about.*

THE CURFEW WAS
YOUR FAULT,
YOU STUDENTS,
YOU RIOTERS,
YOU COMMUNISTS!

Listen, all of you!
It was just a sweet day
of sun and warmth and spring and
it was the beginning of the weekend and
we all wanted to go downtown to celebrate.

Some of us went home for the weekend.
Some of us were downtown looking for girls.
Or guys.
Some of us were looking for a television
so we could watch the NBA finals, because
a television on campus was rare.
Some were headed for a slice at
Big Daddy's Pizza.

Maybe 500 students came to
the noon rally,
but we were a school of over
20,000 students in 1970.
Lots of us had nothing to do with the rally.
Or the violence downtown that night.

*Kids always got a little crazy*
*downtown at the end of the school year*
*when the weather finally got*
*warm and bright.*
*They always swarmed the bars for*
*that 3.2 beer.*
*Remember?*

this is true.

but they were also well-behaved,

before.

They didn't throw beer bottles

at police cars.

We admit, things got out of hand.
Some kids waved down motorists in their cars,
to ask them what they thought about
the invasion of Cambodia.

INCURSION!

We didn't know the motorcyclists who
zoomed around us—

*I knew them—the Chosen Few,*
*they were riding up and down Water Street*
*showing off,*
*doing wheelies, stoppies, and*
*burnouts on their bikes.*
*This dude, Dale, he was like*
*Evel Knievel, jumping over*
*anything in his way.*

Fine, you knew them. (You would.)
Still, we don't know who started the fire.

> it was so loud.
> there was so much shouting.
> and cheering.
> there was a bonfire!

*It was a trash can fire!*
*Dale jumped over it!*

It was festive.
There was a dance party,
right there in the street,
before everything got out of hand.

> OUT OF HAND? IT WAS A RIOT!
> THERE WAS LOOTING!
> YOU BROKE THE LAW!
> DID YOU SEE THE PLATE GLASS
> AT BISSLER'S FURNITURE?
> AT THOMPSON'S DRUG STORE?
> BROKEN INTO A THOUSAND PIECES!
> AND TRASH EVERYWHERE!

> you broke forty-seven windows.
> we counted.

*When the mayor panics*
*because he believes the*
*stupid rumors of*
*Communist outside agitators,*

*calls in the sheriff,*
*CLOSES THE BARS—*

What a mistake.

*—and declares a state of emergency,*
*what do you expect?*

There was not
a large Guard presence
on Friday night.
There was just an advisor.

*Get them out of here!*

THANK GOD FOR THEM!

Okay. *Okay.* Calm down.
You were saying?

*I was saying:*
*What do you expect*
*when you close the bars and*
*force hundreds more of us*
*into the streets and*
*start hurling tear gas at us?*
*What do you expect*
*when the police put on riot gear?*
*You don't think we're going to get*
*a little testy??*

we were scared.

                                                             we owned businesses downtown,

                                                     we'd lived there for generations.

                                                  kent is a small town.

                                            there were only eighteen men

                                      on the entire kent police force—

*Twenty-one!*

                                         and only four on duty

                                           on water street

                                            that night.

                                     there were hundreds of you.

                                            hundreds.

*So your mayor called the governor and*
*he called out his goons and*
*you teargassed us all the way back to campus!*
*You arrested sixty of us!*

                                       it was only eighteen of you.

                                          or was it fifteen?

**We were kids!**

                                    we heard a rumor you were going to

                                    blow up the flour mill on water street.

                                there were 500,000 pounds of flour in there,

                                  the fire would have consumed the town,

                                      you can imagine . . .

**You don't know us very well.**

*Without us—the students, the university—*
*you wouldn't have a town!*

Back. Up.
You are forgetting about Us.
As usual.
Look. At. Us.
Black United Students at Kent State.
Our BUS Brothers and Sisters from Ohio State
Were there on that Friday afternoon
On the Commons.
We held our rally right after yours
To tell you about how the staties
Called in reinforcements
—The Guard—
At Ohio State to deal with
A student strike
Just the day before.
400 of you showed up
At the Victory Bell
To hear them tell you.
They had been asking for
A Black Studies Program.
(So were we.)
They wanted to air their grievances.
(So did we.)
The Guard clubbed them.
Beat them.
Teargassed them.
Then the news came that
Nixon was bombing Cambodia.
4,000 students hit the streets.

At Ohio State

7 Were Shot.

400 Arrested.

100 Injured.

Our Ohio State Brothers

Came to tell you,

Watch Out for the Heat.

Governor Rhodes

Likes to call out the Guard.

OSU Students Were Targeted.

We May Be Next.

You May Be Next.

Especially You Brothers.


*I hardly remember that.*


You wouldn't.


*Hey, some of us are brothers and sisters ...*
*Black is beautiful, baby.*
*We had been protesting!*
*Telling the college to*
*do the right thing—*
*equal housing,*
*programs, clubs, services—*
*we were active as hell*
*with the Kent Chapter of BUS.*


You're interrupting.

some of us in town

were black, too.

there were black citizens in kent.

Governor Rhodes got the press to
Suppress the story at Ohio State.
Hardly anyone remembers it now.
It's a miracle no one got killed.
But everyone remembers Kent State.
Allison. Jeff. Bill. Sandy.
Governor Rhodes could not hide
Murder.

People don't realize how political we were
in the Midwest in the Sixties.
The student body came mostly from Ohio—

*"A suitcase school," they called it—*

—but Kent students were reading
Mao, Lenin, Marx,
and yeah, some of us were in SDS
until it got crazy on campus and
the administration outlawed it.

sds'ers.

COMMUNISTS!

*We weren't Columbia or Berkeley or Harvard*
*but we were paying attention.*
*We knew about free speech and*
*our right to assemble and petition.*
*We'd watched Mario Savio lead the way at Berkeley.*

That's right. In 1964.

Students at Berkeley
upended everything
with civil disobedience
on college campuses—
the Free Speech Movement.

    *Yeah. Mario and Jack and Michael*
    *and Bettina and Jackie—*
    *they got college kids everywhere*
    *all riled up and thinking about change*
    *in this country—*
    *hell, some of us at Kent State went to the*
    *Moratorium Against the War March*
    *on Washington, D.C., the fall of 1969.*

We learned a lot at our kitchen tables . . .

    *But we were in the middle of the country,*
    *nowhere exotic.*
    *No one paid attention to us at Kent State.*

                but they did pay attention to you.
                     they came to speak.
                those civil rights people
              and those socialists, and
                       jerry rubin,
                  head of the yippies,
        —"young independent people . . ."

Youth International Party.

    *More revolutionaries for you—*

Well, people like Abbie Hoffman,
Allen Ginsberg,
they were counterculture people—

they certainly seemed radical.
only weeks before the shooting,
that jerry rubin spoke at kent and told all of you,
"kill your parents. they are your first oppressors."
we read that in the newspaper.

**What does that have to do**
**with our oppression?**

*We heard Jerry.*
*That was cool.*
*Of course we weren't going to*
*kill our parents.*
*You townies gave us*
*no credit for having brains.*

If you'd had half a brain,
you would have gone home
for the weekend
and stayed there.
Most of you lived nearby.
You didn't have to
stay in the dorms.
Do you think we wanted
to be called to Kent?
We were already wearing full riot gear,
just coming off protecting
replacement drivers

in the truckers' strike.

*National Guard scum!*
*You did nothing to protect us!*

YOU GOT WHAT YOU DESERVED!

Wait.

We'd been sleeping in pup tents
in the rain
on a nearby football field,
trying to keep the peace between
these truck-driving supervisors
and the Teamsters
whose deliveries they were making.
It was intense.

*"INTENSE"??? You want to talk "intense"?*

You don't understand.
We were farmers,
rubber plant workers,
autoworkers,
some of us just kids, really—
some of us were students at Kent State
trying to avoid the draft
by joining the Guard.
We weren't soldiers, not really.

*You were murderers.*

THEY WERE GOD-FEARING AMERICANS
SERVING THEIR COUNTRY.
HUSBANDS, SONS, BROTHERS,
NOT HIPPIE RADICALS
TRYING TO TEAR IT APART!
GOD-FEARING AMERICANS!

churchgoers.

schoolteachers.

good parents.

FOR WEEKS WE'D BEEN
CALLING THE POLICE, REPORTING
CARLOADS OF CRAZIES WITH
OUT-OF-STATE LICENSE PLATES.

we may have been misinformed.

There were so many rumors and
false accusations.
You know that now, don't you?

WE KNOW IT WAS ALL YOUR FAULT.

*It always ends like this—*
*Enough!*
*I am exhausted.*
*I hate them.*

Get some rest.

we're not going to talk about the arson?

*No.*

*We're not going to talk about the arson,*
*we're not going to talk about the bayoneting,*
*we're not going to talk about the helicopters—*

my god the helicopters.

*—we're not going to talk about the M1 rifles and*
*we're not going to talk about the SIXTY-SEVEN SHOTS!*

You always get like this,
at this point in the story.
Get some rest.

**You white kids.**
**You get to be exhausted.**
**You get to rest.**

*Hey. We told you:*
*Some of us are black, too.*
*Thousands of us*
*watched this hell unfold.*
*We were horrified.*
*Boys,*
*girls,*
*black,*
*white,*
*faculty,*
*administrators—*

The National Guard.
We were horrified—

*You don't get to be horrified!*

WHAT ABOUT THE TOWN?
YOU THINK WE WEREN'T HORRIFIED?

my grandpa sat at home
with a rifle across his knees
for three solid days,
maybe more.

But most of you are white.
You don't understand your position.
Or ours.

We want to.

*Aren't you exhausted?*

We cannot afford
to be exhausted.

YOU ARE NEVER GOING TO
CHANGE OUR MINDS.

hush.
we don't all think like you,
and we lived in town, too.
it was a tragedy, all of it.

*It's STILL a tragedy.*

WE'RE LEAVING.

We're already gone.
Out the door.
Watch us.


Tomorrow, then.
Tell us tomorrow.
We want to know.


We will tell you
when we are ready.


Tell us, for our friend here,
Who looks like Allison, Bill, Jeff, Sandy.


Or like us.
Or like still others.
We will not be
Overlooked.
We were targeted.
Our friend—
Our friends—
May be next.


*They have been next.*


This is true.


So we'll keep on remembering, then?
For our fine friend here,
who is
new to an old story.

# Saturday
# May 2, 1970

*"What's going on?"*

—Marvin Gaye

We didn't like the curfew.

*We didn't respect it.*

That's true.

YOU DIDN'T RESPECT ANYTHING!
YOU WERE SELFISH.
YOU WERE SUPPOSED TO
RESPECT AUTHORITY.

*Screw authority!*

that's the problem.

*What did you want from us?*
*We were angry.*
*About the police.*
*About the INVASION of Cambodia.*
*About Nixon.*
*About our right to assemble*
*peaceably*
*in downtown Kent*

*being taken away from us*
*because of the bad behavior of*
*a few.*

"BAD BEHAVIOR"?
THAT'S WHAT YOU CALL IT?

You'll remember,
many students went to downtown Kent
on Saturday morning to help clean up.
I think Sandy went, even though
she wasn't even there on Friday night.

*I loved Sandy.*

I know you did.

We couldn't go to town
Saturday after dark
because of the curfew.
We were stuck on campus all night.

*So what could we do*
*with all that anger?*

*"Burn it," someone said.*
*"Burn it to the ground."*
*Not gonna send any more of*
*our Kent State boys*
*to Vietnam!*

who said that?

*Who knows?*

Not everyone at Kent State
was against the war, you know.
Most of the jocks on campus—the athletes—
thought going to Vietnam and supporting
the war was part of our civic, American duty.

*Well, that's what they said.*

Some of us—many of us—
had no opinion!

*Believe me.* Everybody *had an opinion.*

Some of us had fathers there,
brothers,
cousins,
friends.

*But we were politicized by the war!*
*You're not saying we weren't, are you?*

We were politicized by the draft.
That was major.

> We were politicized
> At birth, by white society's
> Reaction to our very existence,
> Then politicized further by
> The Civil Rights Movement and
> Malcolm and

"By Any Means Necessary" and
Vietnam and
Stokely and Eldridge and
Bobby and Huey and—

The Black Panthers.

Of course, man.
What do you think we're saying?
"What Do We Want?"
Everybody Together—
"Black Power!
When Do We Want It?
Now!"

we were scared of you, too.

WE WERE NOT.

you know we were.
they had guns.
they were going to poison
our water supply with lsd.

You got the wrong color people
for that.

*Vicious rumors!*
*You made them up!*
*You just wanted excuses to*
*look big and powerful and*
*in charge. You didn't like*

*our hair. You didn't like*
*our music. You didn't like us*
*questioning your authority.*

"Question Authority."

*You wanted to make us "behave"!*

So we took power,
all of us who wanted it,
on Saturday night.
We weren't very organized,
not the way the press—or the university—

*or the town!*

—thought we were.
Everything was more
spontaneous than that.
But these weren't our first
demonstrations,
protests,
marches,
demands.
We knew how to make noise.

*And you got your wish,*
*didn't you, you townies?*
*You called the governor,*
*who called in the National Guard,*
*all of them this time,*
*not just an advisor.*

*Here they came with their*
*Jeeps and their tear gas and their*
*armored personnel carriers*
*full of soldiers,*
*full of weapons—*
*M1 rifles*
*12-gauge shotguns*
*.45-caliber automatics*
*a machine gun!*

there were more of you

than there were of us.

*We were your* children.
*You said it yourselves.*

you were arsonists.

SOME OF US WERE
THE FIREFIGHTERS
WHO CAME TO
EXTINGUISH THE FIRE
YOU LIT THAT NIGHT.
YOU DON'T THINK WE SAW
WHAT YOU DID?

Coming over the rise
into Kent,
we had the canvas tops down
on our Jeeps
and we could see
the sky was glowing—

eerily silent over there
on the campus,
no sound to go with it at all—
just a brilliant, bright
orange-red glow
against an inky blackness,
like the world was on fire.

it was. our world was on fire.

Long before it burned,
we stood around,
yelling at the ROTC building

you yelled at a building?

Well, yes.
We didn't know what else to do.
We rang the Victory Bell
on the Commons.
We canvassed around campus,
bringing more and more kids
to protest with us . . . or to watch.

*Hundreds, maybe a thousand,*
*maybe more,*
*gathering on the Commons.*
*We tried to decide what to do.*

The Army ROTC building represented
Nixon and his evil,
Vietnam and all the senseless

killing killing killing.
So we marched over there and
threw rocks at it.

                                            Rocks . . .

You had rifles.
We had rocks.

        *It was just an old wooden barracks.*
        *It had been there forever.*

They were going to demolish it
that summer, anyway.

                              THAT'S NO EXCUSE!

There was construction
everywhere on campus,
new buildings going up,
lots of bricks and stones
and gravel to collect and
throw at the building, too—

        *So we did.*
        *Some of us broke the windows.*
        *That musical clink as the glass shattered—*
        *that was satisfying,*
        *so we yelled some more.*
        *"One-two-three-four!*
        *We don't want your fucking war!"*
        *IT FELT GREAT.*

WE HEARD YOU BURNED
AN AMERICAN FLAG.
IS THAT TRUE?

*No!*

Yes.

NO RESPECT.

Things escalated,
the way they do.

> *Some kid tied rags on to a stick*
> *and dipped them into the*
> *gas tank of a motorcycle*
> *in the parking lot,*
> *set the rags on fire, and*
> *hurled them*
> *through a broken window,*
> *where they smoldered.*

Kids ran to the building and
slapped it,
ran back.

you slapped a building . . .

Somebody set the curtains on fire
with a lighter.
It wasn't a big fire.
But the fire department showed up and

45

interrupted our plans.

*So we cut their hoses.*

Yes, we did that.
We used whatever we had.
Some kid had a machete in his dorm room.
Somebody had an ice pick.

where were the university police?

That's a good question.
Where were they?
That's what kids were asking,
especially those who came from the movie
at the student center—

Thunderball. *James Bond*

—to see what was happening
"Where are the cops?
Isn't anyone going to do anything?"

*But then*
*the fire seemed to put itself out.*

So we left the scene,
and so did the fire department,
with their battered hoses.

*But an hour later*
*the building went up in flames.*

Right.
Ammunition in the barracks blew up—
or maybe it was firecrackers that started it,
who knows?—but suddenly
kids came running from all across campus
to see what was happening.

*And then, right on cue:*
*Enter the National Fucking Guard.*
*Rumbling through the front gate of*
*Kent State University.*

Roaring is more like it.
With their bullhorns:
"Back to your dorms!
The university is surrounded!"
Like this was a war zone.

*Which, of course, it was.*

YOU BROUGHT IT ON YOURSELVES.

And they were escorting
the fire department, too.

*Did they swap hoses?*

The governor sent 1,196 of us
to the town of Kent, Ohio,
troops from the 107th Armored Cavalry Regiment
and the 145th Infantry Regiment
with all of our equipment, vehicles,

and three helicopters.

my god the helicopters.

There were many hundreds of us now,
maybe as many as
2,000 gathered on the Commons
near the ROTC building.

There were 850 Guard
assigned to the college,
close as we could tell.

yes. there were about 400 of you in town,
or so said the mayor.
or was it the police chief.
400 of you guarding us now, too.

AND THANK GOD.
PATROLLING OUR STREETS,
CHECKING ON US,
OUR BUSINESSES,
OUR HOMES,
EVEN DIRECTING TRAFFIC!
A CALMING PRESENCE,
THANK YOU!

actually,
it was a little unnerving,
those rifles and uniforms,
heavy boots and helmeted heads,
walking into the bank

with customers standing in line,
or the beauty parlor
with women under the hair dryers,
just . . .
everywhere.

*Never mind the town.*
*It was a crazy scene on campus!*

We screamed and hollered and
chanted and watched
the ROTC building,
that symbol of war and hate,
burn to the ground.

that symbol of war and hate—
the reserve officers' training corps
of the united states military—
has worked to keep you and the world
safe for—

*The heat!*
*The blaze!*
*The power!*
*The* intensity.
*We were transfixed.*
*We'd never been*
*so close*
*to such fire before.*
*The night sky turned orange.*

*It was beautiful.*

We'll never know who
really burned down that building.

WE KNOW.
IT WAS YOU.

*I'll bet it was YOU.*
*And you wanted to pin it on us.*
*You knew that building was going to be*
*torn down that summer.*

WE WOULD NEVER
DESTROY PROPERTY.
WE WOULD NEVER BEHAVE
LIKE YOU DID.

*That's your problem.*
*You sit there in your*
*comfortable homes and*
*eat your comfortable meals and*
*sleep in your comfortable beds and*
*let us fight your uncomfortable war*
*while you make up stories about us to*
*make yourselves feel better*
*for doing nothing*
*while the world goes to hell and*
*you blame anybody but yourselves.*

*You disgust us.*

THEY SHOULD HAVE KILLED MORE OF YOU.

we are not going to go there.

not this time.

Thank you.

continue.

I WILL FINISH!
THE BLAZE WAS UNCONTROLLABLE!
THE FIRE DEPARTMENT CAME WITH
SHERIFF'S DEPUTIES,
HIGHWAY PATROLMEN,
THE NATIONAL GUARD—
WE WERE ALL RISKING OUR LIVES
TO PUT OUT YOUR FIRE!

Not the Guard!
They stood shoulder to shoulder,
bayonets pointed at us.

KEEPING YOU BACK.
KEEPING YOU AWAY.

And then they chased us—
chased us!

*And then the helicopters came.*

my god the helicopters.

No, no, that was Sunday night.

*The helicopters scared us shitless,*
*right overhead, so noisy they*
*drowned out our screaming*
*and so bright their searchlights*
*swept over us and made us look like*
*ants scurrying under their sweep.*
*We began screaming at them,*
*running from them.*
*From YOU.*

Not one of us wanted to be there.


You invaded our campus.
You entered it without even telling
university officials.

Restoring the peace was our goal.

*Bullshit.*

where were the campus police
when the guard appeared?

*Chickenshits.*

DISREPECTFUL!


They turned the campus over to the Guard.

*We had to defend ourselves!*
*That's why there were kids with*
*bows and arrows*

*shooting at the Guard.*

excuse me?

*We ran past the archery hut*
*and saw an opportunity*
*to protect ourselves!*
*Wouldn't you?*

Some of us burned the archery hut.

YOU ADMIT IT!

We burned it so kids would stop
taking the bows and arrows and
trying to kill the cops.

You were all foolish.

*Who says?*

That college didn't belong to you.
It belonged to The Man.
You could have just walked out.
That's what we did.
1968.
The Oakland, California police
Came to recruit
On the Kent campus
Looking to
Hire graduating students
From the law enforcement program.

53

We said No—
They'd tried to kill Huey.
They hated the Panthers.
They targeted Our Black Brothers.
So we protested.
We walked out.
Off campus.
Stayed off, too.
Until the college made them leave.
Until. We. Won.
You think bows and arrows
Would have worked for us?
You think burning buildings
Would have worked for us?
It didn't work for you, either.

That's not the same thing.
You wanted the university to change.

You didn't want that?
Where were they,
These university deans?
Where was your college president?
Dr. Robert White.

*GONE.*

we know for a fact
that bob matson,
the university vice president
of student affairs, met with students on
saturday.

Where were the university police?
Where were the people
Charged with protecting you?

That's a good question.

You were foolish.

*It was mayhem.*
*The police chasing,*
*the students screaming at them,*
*the Guard stomping toward us,*
*the helicopters churning above us,*
*gassing us from the air,*
*ghostly tendrils from the canisters*
*spiraling through the spotlights—*

Listen. That was Sunday night.
The helicopters were on Sunday night.

*The faculty marshals were out there*
*among us (bless them—*
*Dr. Frank, Dr. Kitner, Dr. Duffy, Dr. Lewis)*
*wearing their blue armbands,*
*handing out their flyers—*
> *movie on campus tonight!*
> *curfew downtown!*
> *peace!*
*trying to help us,*
*but what could they do?*

It was good to see them—

*And who was the faculty advisor*
*at the campus radio station?*
*He stayed with the*
*communications students as they*
*tried to let kids know what was happening.*
*Remember?*
*"You're not writing your thesis, for God's sake,*
*you're writing a news bulletin! Get the thing*
*on the air*
*so people know what's happening!"*
*and all the while,*
*the Guard stomping,*
*the ROTC building burning behind us,*
*and the Victory Bell tolling*
*the chaos of the desperate dark.*

**You're romanticizing this.**

We weren't stomping.
We were moving you
back to the dorms,
restoring the peace.

Not so peacefully.

We exercised great restraint.
We didn't want anyone to get hurt.

*LIES!*

We were told you had
targeted the president's home, too,

that it would go up in flames next.

*Wicked rumors.*

Dr. White was
completely ineffectual.
Where was he that night?

iowa. i believe
he'd gone to iowa.

*He wasn't with us.*
*Suddenly we lived in a war zone.*

A WAR ZONE
OF YOUR OWN MAKING.

And we were alone.

# Sunday
# May 3, 1970

*"We're on the eve of destruction."*
—Barry McGuire

You will want to know about Sandy.

*Sandy. My favorite.*

I know.

*Peaches grow in Idaho,*
*California, too,*
*But it would take a state like Iowa*
*to grow a peach like you!*

Was that in her scrapbook?

*She loved her scrapbooks.*
*I think she scrapbooked her entire life.*

She sure packed a lot into a short life,
all those pictures of family vacations,
summer camps, ticket stubs, dances,
all the things she loved.

*Including her sister, Audrey.*
*They were close.*

Yes. And her dad—
he was a Holocaust survivor.
Have I said that before?

*You say it every time.*

Because it's important.
Sandy's parents left Germany
so they could bring up a family
in freedom . . . in America.

*And look what happened.*
*She was just walking to class.*

Don't remind us.
We'd rather think about what a
delightful square she was,
squarely situated in home
and family
and service.
She was going to be a
speech pathologist—

*I remember.*
*"Tan Shoes and Pink Shoelaces" was a*
*favorite song. She liked*
*Dinah Shore and Perry Como,*
*the Carousel Teen Club and*
*Don't Give Up the Ship starring Jerry Lewis—*
*a movie that made her laugh and laugh.*
*It's all in her scrapbooks.*

2 nice
2 be
4 gotten
That was in her scrapbook, too.

> And in her case, it was truly true.
> We saw her on Sunday,
> walking past the
> smoldering ROTC building,
> holding a red ribbon in her hand,
> looking for a dog that was about to have
> puppies—
> she wanted to take care of it.

She found it!
She tied the ribbon around its neck and
asked some of us to adopt it,
because she couldn't keep it.

> Scruffiest dog we ever saw.
> Poor thing.

I wonder what happened to that dog.

> And her puppies.

I'll bet Sandy loved "Bridge over Troubled Water."

> Yeah, she loved Simon & Garfunkel.
> Remember how kids would play their guitars
> to "The Sound of Silence"
> in all those coffeehouses back then?

Makeshift coffeehouses in the
basements of university dorms,
all that candlelight
soaked in smoky incense,
poets and music and prose,
Hermann Hesse, Kahlil Gibran—

Heart of Darkness *and*
The Importance of Being Earnest—

The world of ideas.
Allison loved the world of ideas.
She was an Ohio girl, you know,
from Cleveland, but the family followed
her dad's work at Westinghouse and she graduated
from John F. Kennedy High School in
Silver Spring, Maryland.

*Allison. My favorite.*

I know.

*Did you know she applied only to
Kent State for college? It was the only
place she wanted to go.*

I know.
You tell me that every time.
Her parents were from Kent,
and when they lived in Cleveland, and
Allison and her sister, Laurel, were little,
they'd go on Sunday drives to Kent

and eat at the Robin Hood restaurant.

*Somebody else has a good memory, too.*

We try.

*Well, I remember her at Kent State.*
*She wore love beads one night,*
*a fur coat another, a headband with*
*beat-up jeans and a fringe jacket the next.*
*She was reading*
One Flew Over the Cuckoo's Nest—
*reading ahead in class! She loved it.*

She was opinionated.
She didn't go to town on Friday night,
and she didn't go to the burning of
the ROTC building.
Violence wasn't her bag.

*But she was angry!*
*She had been chased through campus,*
*racing ahead of the tear gas for*
*two nights in a row, and had to*
*spend Saturday night*
*locked in a dorm that wasn't hers.*
*So she was out there on Sunday*
*talking to the Guard.*

We'll get to that.

*She was attractive in every way.*

*I'll bet she charmed that Guard soldier.*
*She attracted people,*
*brought them together.*
*She loved that Melanie song,*
*"Close to It All," remember?*
*Something about tearing down walls and*
*"I want to be close to it all."*

Remember when we all went
sledding on campus
just the winter before?
We hardly knew one another but
Allison brought us together
as we slipped and slid everywhere,
hollering, laughing, piled together—

*like a pack of soft, new puppies.*

She was attractive in every way.

*She was. It was her light.*
*And her light hated the war.*
*She had gravel in her pockets*
*that day,*
*Monday.*
*And she was angry!*
*But that's no reason to*
*shoot someone dead.*

It isn't. You're right.
But this is Sunday.
No one is dying on Sunday.

Jeff hated the war
as much as Allison.

> *Jeff. My favorite.*

I know.

> *Let me tell it!*

Go ahead.

> *Such a light.*
> *He skipped first grade—*
> *that's how brilliant he was.*

Well . . .

> *I'm telling it!*

Go on.

> *He loved math.*
> *And motorcycles.*
> *And the Mets.*
> *And music!*

The Four M's.

> *Ha! Well, he did.*
> *Jefferson Airplane!*
> *Hendrix!*
> *The Dead!*

*And he was a drummer, too.*
*Had a band*
*and a fabulous smile.*

Back to the war . . .

*He hated the war.*
*His brother Russ was three years older*
*and said he'd go to Vietnam if drafted.*
*Jeff said no way would he go,*
*so he became an activist at sixteen*
*and tried to end the war.*
*Protested, marched, wrote poetry, letters,*
*wore a peace ring he bought in New York City.*
*He grew up in the Bronx,*
*then in Plainfield, New York,*
*where he became a bar mitzvah*
*and played with his band.*

He was a DJ, too,
on the college radio station at
Michigan State before
he transferred to Kent.
They called him "Short Mort"
because he was . . . short.
Five feet, six inches tall.

*Short, but strong.*

Unlike Bill, who was six feet, two inches tall
and a basketball player.
Also strong, of course.

*Bill. My favorite.*

I know.

*Anyone who would, at just*
*seventeen years old, sign away*
*ten years of his life to military service!*
*Four in college, to Army ROTC.*
*Four in active military duty.*
*Then two more years to the Army Reserves.*

Yes. No one could say
he tried to avoid the war.
And yet he was against it.

*He was an Ohio boy from Lorain,*
*who first went to college at*
*the Colorado School of Mines*
*to study geology.*
*He'd discovered arrowheads and*
*fossils and historical artifacts*
*with his geologist's pick*
*when he was a boy, and he loved*
*social studies.*

He was a Renaissance Man,
when he was still a boy—
football, baseball, basketball,
poetry, band—

*He was a safety patrol!*

He worked at the Ford Motor assembly plant
and saved enough money to buy himself a
little green Fiat that he drove everywhere.

*He had perfect teeth.*

You pick the strangest details.

*Memory is like that.*
*Selective. Ours.*
*It's what I remember—*
*he had the whitest, prettiest smile.*

He transferred to Kent,
switched his major to psychology,
and decided that the military needed
trained psychologists at the front
as much as they needed riflemen
or chaplains
or medics.

*He read Sigmund Freud and Ray Bradbury*
*and Albert Schweitzer.*
*That's not a strange detail.*

I stand corrected.
There are no strange details.

*Okay! He once won a bar bet*
*from a guy who didn't believe*
*Bill could recite,*
*chronologically and in sequence,*

*all twelve Rolling Stones album titles*
*plus all songs on those twelve albums*
*in numerical order.*

What was the prize?
Free Rolling Rock?

*Twenty-five bucks!*

You're romanticizing them.

It's impossible not to.
Wouldn't you?

We have. Yes.
It's hard to think of
Martin or Malcolm or
The Many Others—
Especially Our Young—
As just people
When they have been
Taken from us
So violently.

We're eulogizing them.
There's a difference.

*It's only Sunday.*
*They're not dead yet.*

we would like equal time.
we have been waiting our turn.
patiently.

Of course.

*Of course NOT!*
*Let me tell you why.*
*In Kent, whose streets run right*
*to the gates of our university,*
*you welcomed the enemy on Sunday.*

*And here's what*
*Governor James Rhodes said*
*about us—*

we remember.
of course.
we were there,
at the fire station,
listening.

*"We're asking the legislature*
*that any person throwing a*
*rock, brick, or stone*
*at a law enforcement agency of Ohio—*
*a sheriff, policeman, highway patrolman,*
*or national guardsman*
*becomes a felony . . .*
*We are going to eradicate this problem . . .*
*These people just move from one campus*
*to another and terrorize a community.*
*They're worse than the 'Brown Shirt'*
*and the communist element*
*and also the 'night riders' in the Vigilantes.*
*They're the worst type of people*

*that we harbor in America.*
*And I want to say that they're not going to*
*take over the campus . . .*
*the campus now is going to be*
*part of the County and the State of Ohio.*
*There is no sanctuary for these people . . .*
*It's over with in Ohio."*

Did you memorize that?

*You bet I did.*
*He said more than that. He said*
*the Guard would use every weapon*
*available to eradicate the problem.*
*To eradicate US.*

Nixon hated us like that.

*I've memorized what he said, too.*

Of course you have.

*Listen—*
*I can even sound like him:*
*"You see these bums, you know,*
*blowing up the campuses. Listen, the boys*
*that are on the college campuses today are*
*the luckiest people in the world, going to the*
*greatest universities, and here they are,*
*burning up the books. Storming around*
*about this issue. You name it.*
*Get rid of the war, there'll be another one."*

That was in *The New York Times*.

*Did you hear the rest?*
*"Then out there we have kids who are*
*just doing their duty.*
*They stand tall and they are proud.*
*I'm sure they are scared . . .*
*But when it really comes down to it,*
*they stand up, and boy you have to*
*talk up to those men.*
*They are going to do fine and*
*we have to stand in back of them."*

MR. NIXON
—OUR PRESIDENT—
WAS RIGHT.
WE STOOD BEHIND THOSE BOYS.
NOT YOU.

*He called us bums!*

YOU *WERE* BUMS!

Listen.
Some of us—
on campus—
believed in the war.
Believed we were furthering
the cause of democracy
in Vietnam.
Believed the Viet Cong's
weapons were hidden in

74

Cambodia. We needed to
destroy them in order to
save lives.

Some of us
hated what the rabble-rousers
were doing to our campus,
let's be honest.
Some of us weren't protesting.
Some of us were studying for exams,
helicopters whirring and spotlights
blasting through our dorm room windows.

> *He called us bums!*
> *For disagreeing with him!*
> *Disagreeing is our*
> *constitutional right!*

burning buildings is
more than disagreeing.

### DESTROYING PROPERTY IN OUR TOWN IS MORE THAN DISAGREEING.

beautiful little kent,
quiet and tree-lined,
the tree city, with
black squirrels and lilac gardens
that perfumed the air,
everywhere,
every day of spring.

                                              our families
                                   went back generations here,
                                           salt of the earth,
                                               war heroes:
                                               world war I,
                                              world war II,
                                           the korean war,
                                           flags everywhere,
                           apple pies cooling on windowsills,
                                 baseball games in the park,
                                       a bustling little city
                                     full of hardworking,
                                    churchgoing families,
                                    pot luck dinners and
                                      fireman's carnivals,
                                          young captains
                                          of little industries
                                               growing up
                          around kitchen tables with
                                 clean-scrubbed faces—

You're romanticizing.
All those white faces.

                                              we had black faces, too,
                                                       still do.

Show us one Black face
Who was
A Captain of Industry.

You're losing the thread.

That is the thread.

The point is,
we had to live together,
somehow.

> beautiful little kent,
> with its river and
> railroad tracks,
> inseparable from kent state,
> the university that
> enriched our culture
> with its music and drama,
> with its fine colleges of business,
> journalism, nursing, speech.
> what happened to you,
> you students?

The Ohio National Guard
happened to us.

*You should have
turned around and
gone home!*

We were following orders.

*Sunday was peaceful!
Allison caught the lilac that
a Guard officer yanked out of
a soldier's gun barrel and she
called after him,*

*"What's the matter with peace!*
*Flowers are better than bullets!"*

She was attractive in every way.

some of us might have seen her.
some of us came to campus to see
what was going on.
we were curious,
we came in our cars,
after church,
on a sunday afternoon lark,
with our families,
driving right through
the center of it all,
to see the burned building,
to see the encampment,
the weapons, the soldiers
everywhere,
our kids hanging out
the open car windows,
staring.

Yes. We saw you.

there was a smiling girl
with a clutch of daisies.
she silently passed them out,
one by one,
pressed them into our hands
through the open car windows,
to whoever would take one.

Like Allison, a flower child.
Peace, brother.
Peace, sister.

*Bunches of us milled around*
*on Sunday morning, too,*
*staring at the charred ROTC building,*
*talking softly with the soldiers.*

That part was nice.
Some of us were your age.
Don't you understand?
We were forced to be there.

Some of us could see that.
Remember the girl who was dancing
and asking you your names and where
you were from?
Remember the girl who stuck the
lilac in that soldier's rifle barrel?

*I thought it was Sandy.*
*She loved lilacs.*

Sandy was looking for her stray dog.

i wonder what happened
to those puppies.

*See? It was peaceful.*

*It was a sit-in!*
*We staged a sit-in!*
*It was peaceful.*
*We were singing*
*"Give Peace a Chance."*

We gathered at the Prentiss Gate
at the corner of Main and Lincoln.
We sat right in the street
and blocked traffic
and demanded to speak
to President White.
We wanted the Guard off campus.
We knew President White
was back from
wherever he had gone.

he'd gone to iowa.

*But he never showed up!*

Neither did the mayor—

*LeRoy Satrom,*
*his dis-honor,*
*who'd panicked*
*and asked the governor*
*to send in the Guard*
*in the first place!*

80

HE HAD ONLY BEEN MAYOR
FOR FIVE MONTHS!
YOU FORGET—
HE'D HEARD THE SDS WAS
BRINGING IN
OUTSIDE AGITATORS.
HE WAS DOING HIS DUTY
BY THE CITIZENS OF KENT.

*The agitated chief of police*
*told him that rumor.*
*And he believed it!*

you'd have believed it, too,
if you had been us.

*He was a pissant!*

We wanted someone to listen to us.
The Kent chief of police,
somebody—
there were
hundreds and hundreds of us
sitting at the gate,
waiting,
and you had promised
to come talk to us.

the army had taken over.
governor rhodes gave the guard
full command—
they were your law and order now.

and they were instructed:
no more assemblies on campus,
peaceful or otherwise.

Vice President Matson told us
peaceful assemblies were lawful.
We were peaceful
sitting at the Prentiss Gate,
hundreds of us.
singing, chanting,
asking for a dialogue.

*PIGS OFF CAMPUS!*

not so peaceful.

*You turned our campus
into an armed camp!*

We were following orders,
and the orders were to
form a straight line,
move forward with fixed bayonets
in a steady cadence,
to move you back onto campus,
to get you to disperse
and go back to your dorms.

*We didn't want to disperse.*

Nevertheless.

We dispersed.
We fanned out
across the Commons
in the dark.
Someone began ringing
the Victory Bell in earnest.
Over and over and over.
And over.

That damned bell.

Then, suddenly,
helicopters hovered overhead,
their blades stuttering
like racing heartbeats above us,
the wind underneath them
blowing us to pieces
while their spotlights
swept over us,
pinpointing our
terror, our outrage.

*That's right, it was*
*Sunday night.*
*The helicopters were*
*on Sunday night.*

my god the helicopters.
they flew over our homes
all night.
our children slept with us,
fear in their hearts.
and ours.

IT WAS THE AGITATORS!
CHIEF THOMPSON TOLD
MAYOR SATROM THAT
THE WEATHERMEN
HAD BEEN SPOTTED
ON CAMPUS!

You were misinformed.

we held our children close.

And you Guardsmen,
you kept marching.
Demons in uniforms,
wearing helmets and
heavy boots,
carrying rifles that were
pointed at us,
stomping,
like monsters out of
the Twilight Zone.

We weren't monsters.

*You were. Are.*

There were thousands of you
out there by now
in the dark,
on the Commons
on Blanket Hill,
watching, screaming,

"Here we come!"
and we knew
we were outnumbered.
What were we going to do?

*We were students!*
*You chased us across campus,*
*to our dorms, then*
*you locked us in!*

And if you caught us,
you bayoneted us.
Some of us went
to the hospital.

*Most of us didn't.*

It was about more than
the war now.
Kids who weren't even
protesting the war protested
YOU on our campus.

*You stuck us!*
*Stuck us like the pigs you are!*
*Stabbed us in the back!*
*We bled!*

We protected plenty of you, too,
let you slip between us,
back to your dorms,
out of the way,

                                          bystanders
                                    caught in the middle.
                              Nobody talks about that.
                              You all conveniently
                                          forget that.
                              You forget any kindness.

**Murder wipes out kindness.**

*I'm ready to talk about the killings.*

                              YOU WON'T CHANGE OUR MINDS.

We know.

*And you won't change ours.*

But we are not remembering for you.
We are remembering for our friend here,
who is not unlike
Allison, Jeff, Sandy, and Bill.

     *Or*
     *Alan,*
     *Tom,*
     *Joe,*
     *John,*
     *Dean,*
     *Doug,*
     *Jim,*
     *Robbie,*
     *and*

*Don.*

*Nine were wounded, remember.*

> Or Phillip Lafayette Gibbs
> And
> James Earl Green
> At Jackson State
> Eleven days later.
> We want to talk about them.

We will.
We will talk about all of us.

> *Including our friend here—*
> *are you still with us?*

INSERT YOUR NAME HERE.

# Monday
# May 4, 1970

*"Four dead in Ohio"*

—Crosby, Stills, Nash & Young

William Knox Schroeder, age 19,
wore his Brian Jones corduroy bell-bottom pants,
an orange-and-purple-striped shirt,
and his grandfather's beloved denim railroad jacket
as he walked from class
to see what was happening on the Commons,
holding his textbook.
He was 382 feet away from the soldiers when they fired.

**INSERT YOUR NAME HERE.**

Allison Beth Krause, age 19,
wore jeans and blue sneakers,
and had clipped her long dark hair
on top of her head.
The word KENNEDY splashed
across her T-shirt.
She carried a wet cloth
to use against the tear gas filling the air,
and tore it to share with another student.
She was 343 feet away from the soldiers when they fired.

**INSERT YOUR NAME HERE.**

Sandra Lee Scheuer, age 20,
was walking to her speech class.
She wore a red sweater.
It was the day of her parents' wedding anniversary.
She had sent them a card,
to arrive on this day.
She was 390 feet away from the soldiers when they fired.

**INSERT YOUR NAME HERE.**

Jeffrey Glenn Miller, age 20,
had talked with his mother
by phone the night before.
"Don't worry. I'm not going to get hurt.
You know me . . . I won't get that involved."
He called his mother that morning and told her
he was going to go to the rally,
was that okay? She told him
she trusted his judgment.
He was 265 feet away from the soldiers when they fired.

**INSERT YOUR NAME HERE.**

What happened?
What is the evidence?
What was the sequence of events?
The narrative continues to be a lived experience.
The thing to do now is listen.

HELL NO WE WON'T GO!
HELL NO WE WON'T GO!
HELL NO WE WON'T GO!

Rallies were banned.
No they weren't.
Yes they were.
The Guard said they were.
President White said they weren't.
Then he said they were.
Or did he?

The university printed flyers saying rallies were banned.
Students handed out flyers saying they weren't.
We went to the rally.
By noon, there were 2,000 of us.


There were 113 Guardsmen on the Commons
at this time:
51 from Company A of the First Battalion,
    145th Infantry Regiment;
36 from Company C of the First Battalion,
    145th Infantry;
16 from Troop G, Second Squadron,
    107th Armored Cavalry Regiment;
and 10 officers.
Troops were led by
General Canterbury,
Lieutenant Colonel Fassinger,
and Major Harry Jones.

Students rang the Victory Bell and we came
and kids began the usual speeches
denouncing the war, hating Nixon, sprinkling in
communism, racism, capitalism, sexism,
and then the question:
Are we going to join the national student strike?

Cheering, yelling, chanting.

GUARD OFF CAMPUS!
GUARD OFF CAMPUS!
GUARD OFF CAMPUS!

The Guard spread across the back of the Commons,
near the burned-out ROTC building.
They donned their gas masks.
They got their orders from Colonel Fassinger to
"lock and load."


Some of us saw them loading their M1 rifles.
Those bullets were three inches long, man.
*Live ammunition.*


There was a sign in the window of a freshman girls' dorm:
THANK YOU, N.G.


We didn't believe they had real bullets.


You see a man wearing a uniform
carrying a rifle and
you don't think it's loaded?!?


Such confusion.


*"There can be no excuse*
*for General Robert H. Canterbury's decision*
*to forcibly disperse an entirely peaceful and legal rally*
*on Monday, just 30 minutes before the shooting,*
*remarking as he did so,*
*'These students are going to have to find out*
*what law and order is all about.'"*
—The New York Times


They rode around us in a Jeep,
campus police and the Guard,

with a bullhorn,
                    ordering us to disperse.
            "Leave this area immediately!
            Please, for your own safety!"


            POWER TO THE PEOPLE!


            All Power to All the People.

We would not be moved.
So they teargassed us.
            Yellow smoke curling through the midday sunshine on a breeze,
                canisters landing at our feet, the gas choking us,
                    tears streaming down our burning faces,
                        some kids wearing bandannas like cowboys,
                            some kids picking up the canisters,
                                throwing them back at the Guard,
                                    one kid standing there,
                                        defiantly waving
                                            a black flag,
                                            daring them
                                            to come get him.
Kids with cameras snapping pictures.
            Kids throwing rocks and hitting the Jeep,
                hitting the police.
                    The police made a retreat,
                        we cheered.
                                But they just regrouped.


And here came the soldiers,
marching across the wide-open Commons,
shoulder to shoulder,

in a skirmish line,
fixed bayonets,
gas masks,
rifles locked, loaded.
Coming for us.

Dissent will get you killed.

We didn't believe they had real bullets.

If you were white, you had the privilege of believing that.

We knew they had real bullets.
If you were black,
that privilege
evaporated.
A soldier holding a gun aimed at you
had real bullets
and would shoot you.
BUS told black students
to stay away
from the Commons
on May 4.

Most of them did.

The M1 is a high-velocity weapon.
Its bullets have a horizontal range of
almost two miles.
If they decided to shoot,
you weren't getting away.

We threw whatever we had at them.
 Rocks.
  Sticks.
   Stones.
    Names.
     Curses.
      Screams.

GUARD OFF CAMPUS!

They kept coming,
 shoulder to shoulder,
  bayonets pointed,
   grenadiers firing volleys of tear gas
   into the crowd, using M79 grenade launchers,
   the gas spiraling around us and forcing some of us
   to retreat up Blanket Hill and spill over it on either side
   of Taylor Hall, and down the other side of the hill,
   onto the veranda of Taylor Hall and
   into the Prentiss Hall parking lot.

   Company C silently blocked students from going back
   to the Commons on their side of Taylor Hall.

On the opposite side of Taylor Hall,
 77 Guardsmen from Company A and Troop G
  advanced on students with tear gas and bayonets,
   and drove them over the hill.

The Guardsmen followed them, in the bright May sunshine,
 Company A to the left of Taylor Hall,
 blocking students from reentering the Commons.
 Troop G to the right of Taylor Hall and

into a practice football field,
where they huddled for ten minutes,
trying to figure out what to do next.
Waiting for orders.

There was nowhere to go,
and what else was there to do?

For ten minutes, while troops waited for orders,
we threw rocks and epithets,
angry-angry-angry—full of rage!—at the Guard.

Jeff threw rocks.

Allison screamed in protest.

GUARD OFF CAMPUS!
Where were our protectors?

Rocks fell short—the Guardsmen were too far away—
but the noise was deafening.
Some of the Guardsmen threw rocks back.

The kid with the black flag
followed the Guard onto the practice field
and waved his flag at them in fury.

Where were our protectors?

Troop G knelt and aimed their rifles at him
and others for a long moment,
but no one fired.

General Canterbury walked from his position at the other side of Taylor Hall with
Company C, through the crowd of students, and onto the practice field, where he
huddled with Major Jones. Then he ordered his troops to retrace their steps up
Blanket Hill and go back to the ROTC building on the far side of the Commons.

*"My purpose was to make it clear*
*beyond any doubt to the mob*
*that our posture was now defensive*
*and that we were clearly returning to the Commons,*
*thus reducing the possibility of injury to either soldiers or students."*
—General Robert Canterbury

The Guard left the practice field and
marched, in a V-formation,
back up Blanket Hill,
toward the Pagoda structure
and the Commons.
We thought it was over.
Some of us started to leave.
Kids screamed WE WON!
Kids were ebullient!
We thought it was over

when suddenly—

28 Guardsmen—mostly in Troop G—
turned as one man and began to fire.

13 seconds.
67 shots.

The campus was a war zone
and American students were the enemy.

"The bullets just went everywhere."
                *pop! pop! pop!*
                                dive for cover!
                                        hit the ground!
                                                behind a tree!
                                                        between parked cars!
                                                                hurry!

Don't run! They're blanks!

WE DIDN'T BELIEVE THEY HAD BULLETS.

                                My God! They're killing us!
                                There's blood everywhere!

How young and innocent we were.

I heard the volley—
I grabbed her—
we dove for cover—

        I screamed STAY DOWN!
        It's buckshot!
        But it wasn't.

                        The sound split my eardrums.
                        I turned to run
                        and the face of the boy behind me
                        exploded,
                        flesh and blood and bone.

        Sunlight glinted off the cartridges flying through the air,

Officers screamed
CEASE FIRE!
CEASE FIRE!
CEASE FIRE!

We were on the ground.
I had my arm around her.
She was motionless.

Joe was flipping them the bird, defiant,
as the Guard turned and aimed their weapons,
then *pop-pop-pop!* and he was on the ground,
screaming,
      bleeding,
          writhing,
his pain spilling over us,
blood ballooning inside his jeans.
"My God, they shot me!"
Then shouts:
"Unzip his pants! Get them off!"
Somehow we did.
There was a hole blown out of him.

Brother Fargo,
a black brother from BUS,
came to help
despite the BUS warning to stay away.

A bullet went straight through
the metal sculpture
on the hill,
producing a rusty red puff of smoke.

A bullet went through the wrist
of the kid with the black flag as he
dove behind a tree, which
took more shots meant for him,
that beautiful tree,
its bark spraying off in bursts as the
bullets thwacked against it.

We grabbed one another,
          pushed one another to the ground,
              rolled for cover—
              STAY DOWN!
                    But some of us ran.

Groups of people
kneeling, shot, bleeding.
And the Guard marched away,
over the hill,
to the Commons.
We were left to tend to ourselves,
alone.

"Somebody call an ambulance!"

        It was pandemonium.

"Sandy, it's over. Let's go."
But she didn't move.
There was a lot of blood.

We moved her, others tried to help,
including a Vietnam vet.

We tried to stop the bleeding
but it wouldn't stop.

                    Sandy Scheuer died
                of a gunshot wound to her neck
                that severed her carotid artery.
            She bled out on the ground of her campus.

"WHEN ARE THEY COMING TO HELP?"

            We tried to help him.
            I held his hand.
            He squeezed back and stared at me.
            He was silent.
            I whispered, "Stay with me,"
            as his eyes closed and he let go.

They were running away, hand in hand,
Allison and her boyfriend, Barry.
They took cover between cars
in the parking lot.

She had already been shot,
the bullet slicing through
her upper left arm and
tunneling into her left side
where it fragmented on impact.
The bullet left a huge exit wound.
Blood poured onto the asphalt.
Barry held her in his arms
while they waited for an ambulance.

Allison Krause died
from the impact of a bullet
that entered her left arm and side,
where it shattered,
causing massive internal damage as it
ripped through most of her major organs.

Bullets whizzed past our heads.
We saw someone get shot in the chest.
The impact of the bullet lifted him
off the ground and
threw him back down, like a rag doll.

We surrounded him.
"Stand back! Give him room to breathe!"
There was a spreading bloodstain on his chest.

Bill Schroeder died
from a single gunshot wound.
The bullet entered his left back at the seventh rib,
piercing his left lung,
and some fragments of the bullet
exited from the top of his left shoulder.
He died an hour later while in a hospital
undergoing surgery.
He was walking to class
after a meeting with his ROTC advisor.

Jeff had been protesting
since he was sixteen years old.

He wore his peace ring,

the one he'd bought
in the Village in New York City.

He had been throwing rocks
at the Guard.
He had been chanting and screaming.
He'd promised his mother he'd be careful.
He had been exercising his
First Amendment rights.
And they shot him.

Jeff Miller died
of a single gunshot wound.
The bullet entered his mouth
and exited the base of his skull.
His brain matter and part of his skull
lay on the ground next to him.
He died instantly.

Some of us were frozen in place,
in shock.
Some of us knelt by the wounded
with comfort and first aid.

We tried to stanch wounds with
our T-shirts, rags we'd brought with us
for tear gas attacks,
anything we had.
Many of us joined hands
and formed protective circles
around the wounded
while we waited for help.

Some of us rushed up over Blanket Hill, past Taylor Hall,
and back down the other side of Blanket Hill and staged a
sit-in on the grassy slope near the Victory Bell, and we stayed,
even when we were told to disperse.

We were angry,
we were shocked,
we were injured,
we were violated.
Our friends lay wounded, dying, and dead
on the other side of Blanket Hill,
and we would not be moved.

The Guard made ready again.
Locked and loaded.

Professor Frank pleaded with the Guard to stop.
"We have orders," they said.
"Over my dead body," he told them.

And he turned to us:

"I don't care whether you've never listened
to anyone before in your lives.
I am begging you right now.
If you don't disperse,
they're going to move in,
and it can only be a slaughter.
Would you please listen to me?
Jesus Christ, I don't want to be part of this."

The ambulances arrived.

The police arrived.
The news cameras arrived.
Parents arrived.
The university was closed.
We heard the truth in Dr. Frank's voice.

We needed to count the dead and wounded.
We needed to show up for them.
We needed to tell our parents we were alive.

But this fight was not over.
It would never be over.

We stood up.
We looked around us at the carnage.
And almost without knowing it,
we made a plan for the future.
Because one thing we knew for sure:

They did not have to die.

# elegy

Every May 4 we meet,
the living and the dead,
right here, on this field,
this Commons,
near the Victory Bell,
at this university,
in memory.

> *Now we know,*
> *there were no outside agitators,*
> *there were no Weathermen,*
> *no SDS'ers*
> *from somewhere else.*

we are still unsure about that.

You are unsure because
you want to be.
Because you can't

face the fact that you—
your government, your sworn-to-protect
guardians of democracy—
killed us,
your children,
because you didn't like
what we were doing.
Not because we broke the law,
but because we exercised our rights
as American citizens,
and you can't live with that truth,
so you make up a story.

we believe our story
is the truth.

And that is the tragedy.

*"The indiscriminate firing of rifles
into a crowd of students
and the deaths that followed
were unnecessary, unwarranted, and inexcusable."*
—The President's Commission on Campus Unrest, 1970

*You make heroes out of oppressors.*

LIKE WHO?

Look it up:
The Boston Massacre.
The Trail of Tears.

*(Christopher Columbus)*

I DON'T UNDERSTAND
HOW THIS IS THE SAME
AS WHAT HAPPENED
AT KENT STATE?

*Understand your history.*
*You lie*
*in order to get*
*what you want.*

give us an example.

SLAVERY.
LYNCHING.
Racial Profiling.
Mass Incarceration.

we don't do that in kent.

Understand your history.
As a country
Our government has
Misused its power
And its privilege
To get what those in power
Want.

what do they want?

More power.

Look it up:
Wounded Knee.
The Dakota Access Pipeline.
Separating families at our borders.

we can't even begin
to form an argument here,
you won't let us.

*And that's the point.*

we need a chance to talk, too.

You are right.
Go ahead.

LET'S SAY,
FOR THE SAKE
OF ARGUMENT,
THAT YOU ARE RIGHT.
WHAT ARE WE SUPPOSED TO DO
ABOUT THAT?

We want you to listen.
No one listened when
the Guard roared onto our campus.
No one listened when
we asked for a dialogue.
Over 58,000 Americans died
in Vietnam
because our government
would not listen

to the overwhelming
majority of Americans
who were against the war.
Including us.

                                                you're saying
                                    everyone needs to be heard.


When the State silences
freedom of assembly
and freedom to dissent,
it silences the people
it is sworn to protect.
We need you to listen.


                                            then you must not
                                            silence us, either.

                                            when you silence us,
                                            you give permission to
                                            others to do the same.
                                    silencing opposing opinions
                                            encourages people to
                                                    take the law
                                            into their own hands.


You're talking about
lone gunmen.


                                                            yes.


Hate crimes.

                                                        yes.
                                              we hate them, too.

Citizens
should be safe in
nightclubs,
synagogues,
churches,
outdoor spaces,
public places,
their own homes.

    *And at school.*
    *Columbine,*
    *Nickel Mines,*
    *Virginia Tech,*
    *Newtown,*
    *Parkland—*

                                                  we agree.

                                          **WE AGREE.**

    **And South Carolina State**
    **In Orangeburg, 1968.**

*And at*
*Kent State University.*
*May 4, 1970.*

    **Don't forget those who were**
    **Suddenly**

Individually
Targeted.
Sandra Bland.
Freddie Gray.
Philando Castile.
Michael Brown.
Oscar Grant.
Eric Garner.
Tamir Rice.
Phillip Lafayette Gibbs and
James Earl Green
At Jackson State College,
Eleven days after Kent State,
May 15, 1970.

There are So Many.
We are only
Scratching the surface.

We will add:
Allison Krause.
Jeffrey Miller.
Bill Schroeder.
Sandy Scheuer.

*May they rest in peace—*

WE WOULD LIKE TO
REST IN PEACE ONE DAY
AS WELL.

WE WANT TO SAY
AMEN TO THAT.

then say amen.

*May they rest in power.*

When the Power of Love
Overcomes the Love of Power
The world will know Peace.

*Jimi!*

perhaps that is true.

*It is.*

There you go.

AMEN.

*You're giving Jimi*
*an Amen.*
*I like it.*

But our friend Mario Savio,
who led the way for us,
in Berkeley, so long ago,
is also right.

*Allow me:*

*"There's a time when the operation of the machine becomes*
*so odious, makes you so sick at heart, that you can't take*
*part! You can't even passively take part! And you've got to*
*put your bodies upon the gears and upon the wheels . . . upon*
*the levers, upon all the apparatus, and you've got to make it*
*stop! And you've got to indicate to the people who run it, to the*
*people who own it, that unless you're free, the machine will be*
*prevented from working at all!"*

That's what we did
at Kent State.
We will continue
to hold our government
accountable.

*Accountable.*

**Accountable.**

what do you intend to do?

We intend to follow
their lead:
Allison, Bill, Sandy, and Jeff.

*We intend to live good lives.*

We intend to be informed citizens.

*We intend to be good friends.*

We intend to stand up for what is right.

*We intend to call out what is wrong.*

We intend to use our privilege
and our talents
and our energy
to make this democracy work.

*To change this country.*

**We intend to be
The conscience
Of America.**

*It has always been the young
who are our champions
of justice.
Who stand at the vanguard
of change.*

And that's what
we invite you to do,
our new friend.
You have come
all this way with us.
You are still here.
Good.

*We hope you're
on fire
for change.*

*for hope.*
*for love.*

**Souls on fire.**

Here is all you have to do:

**INSERT YOUR NAME HERE.**

# a note about May 4 and this story

It is a profound privilege to spend time with the dead. It is a daunting proposition to write about their deaths.

You want to get it right. You research and interview and read and take notes and write drafts, all of it, over and over, and you go to the place they were murdered and you stand on the earth where they fell and you feel something visceral move within you. Why is that?

Maybe it's because the spring night is soft and the candles flicker in their paper cups and the walk around the campus perimeter with the others was long and full of shadows, and now, at the midnight gathering, many voices are chanting in unison the Lord's Prayer (Bill was Catholic), followed by students from the campus Hillel—and many others—reciting the Kaddish (Allison, Sandy, and Jeff were Jewish).

The experience moves your heart to tears for lives cut short, for lives forever altered, for lives forever damaged—and for a country forever scarred—as the prayers end and the mourners silently fashion their candles into a giant glimmering peace sign of white paper cups on the ground near the marker, under the tree, in the parking lot where so much tender blood was shed.

Maybe it's the gentleness of strangers who are there with you, in the darkness, that causes you to cry. Surrounding you are ghosts of the dead, yes, the dead you have been living alongside for years, as you got to know them and fell in love with them and became so devoted to them, as if you had really known them.

The strangers with you, though, are living bodies of all ages, including former classmates of the dead, their hair graying with age, their faces somber with remembrance. Current students, fresh with youthful energy, are also part of the gathering, as are those who have traveled to Kent State University on a May weekend, to honor the fallen and try to make sense of what happened. I am one of them.

Maybe the tears reach your lips and taste salty as you watch the all-night vigil begin, as four lantern-holding sentries stand, silently, each in one of the four marked places where war and death visited Kent State in 1970, courtesy of our American government.

Those four sentries will be spelled in intervals through the night by four more, and four more, every May 4, in cold, rain, wind, snow, or on balmy, starry nights, year after year after year, until noon that day when the Victory Bell will ring to call them to order with everyone who has gathered on the Commons to honor Sandy, Jeff, Allison, and Bill, and to recite the chronology of events, the memory of May 4, of what transpired that weekend, of what really happened.

Maybe that visceral feeling you have standing there in the dark with the memories of Sandy, Jeff, Allison, and Bill on your heart is the realization—because you have done your homework by now—that you will never be able to do their stories justice, or tell definitively what happened, because there is so much unknown, or disputed, or misremembered and misconstrued.

With any story, with any life, with any event whether joyous or tragic, there is so much more to know than the established, inadequate norm: There will be as many versions of the truth as there are people who lived it.

And there is no May 4 chronology recited at the yearly commemoration for the townspeople of Kent, or the Ohio National Guard soldiers, or for the students who were there but who were not killed or wounded. Townspeople, soldiers, students . . . of course they have stories to tell. Of course they have memories and their subsequent interpretations of facts. Of course they have opinions and personal experiences of May 4.

And, of course, they are all important, and part of the whole. So how do you tell the story of what happened?

You employ the facts as you can confirm them, and you mine those memories—the collective memory—as best you can. You make up nothing. You include faulty memory (Were there helicopters on Saturday night? Were there firecrackers thrown at the ROTC building? Who really set the fire? Were there outside agitators? Was there an order given to fire on May 4?), and you include opinion ("They should have killed more of them!") from letters sent to the local newspaper.

You allow all remembrances from the rich vein of oral histories collected and stored at the May 4 Special Collections Archive at Kent State, even when they are contradictory memories, because those memories are true to their storytellers, and all voices must be heard, even those whose opinions you don't agree with. Your job is to dig and discover and structure a narrative truth you can share.

In his book *Collective Memory and the Historical Past*, Jeffrey Andrew Barash writes that we honor great tragedies by never forgetting, that our social cohesion as a human society depends on our storytelling. It depends on our remembering, passing on what we remember, saving it, and honoring it.

So that's what you do. You serve. You bring your audience close, and you whisper in their ears: *Here is what I heard. Here is what I found. Here is what happened.*

You treat the past as a lived experience, which it was, and at the same time you try to separate historical facts from the mythology surrounding them. And to do that, you ask for help.

You can find so much about the May 4 massacre at Kent State just by entering those words into a search engine online. That's how I started, long ago. In a way, I started researching this story long before I consciously knew I would write about it or even become a writer, long before there was an internet, as I was a sixteen-year-old high school student on May 4, 1970. Allison, Jeff, Sandy, and Bill were killed three days before my seventeenth birthday. The news was unbelievable and everywhere, all we could talk about in school and at dinner tables around the country. I will always remember how the shock of that event stayed with me through that birthday week, and became a part of the fabric of my coming of age. The earthquake of its enormity has never left me.

I wanted this book to be as quietly eloquent as possible, about so devastating a moment in our history, so I purposely chose to invite you to take this story further in whatever ways you felt led, by looking online or by reading the many print resources that exist about May 4, or by visiting Kent State University yourself; more about that below.

One of the most helpful factual resources for me was *This We Know: A Chronology of the Shootings at Kent State, May 1970* by former Kent State students Carole Barbato and Laura Davis, and Mark Seeman. Carole Barbato was a friend of both Sandy and Bill. Laura Davis was a Kent State student in 1970 and a witness to the shootings.

For over a decade, both Drs. Barbato and Davis taught the course "May 4 1970 and Its Aftermath" at Kent State. They were co-creators of the Kent State University May 4 Visitors Center and May 4 Walking Tour. They also, along with archaeologist and anthropology professor Mark Seeman and sociology professor Jerry Lewis, co-authored the nomination to place the May 4 site on the National Register of Historic Places.

Laura Davis still lives in Kent, and is professor emeritus of English. She was generous to a fault with a writer who didn't even know what questions to ask when we first met; there was just so much material to make sense of, and I couldn't figure out a way into the story.

Dr. Davis spent patient time with me helping me understand the landscape of the story. She also shared with me the 108-page National Historic Landmark nomination, which is filled with contextual and factual details about the May 4 weekend as well as the long arm of history, dissent, and government violence that Kent State became a part of on May 4, 1970. I could not have written the story without her.

The cultural, geographical, and political context I needed to tell this story came from the generosity of many, including Tom Grace, whose correspondence challenged me to make the vital and very real connections between "state violence, as versus the epidemic of violence by lone gunmen," which I had been trying to do.

Dr. Grace was wounded on May 4, 1970, when a bullet shattered his left foot and ankle. He became a social worker, a union representative, and a history professor, and has authored one of the best books I read about "The Kent State Killings," as he corrected me in my first email to him. The book is *Kent State: Death and Dissent in the Long Sixties* and is well worth your time.

I would not have had access to these wonderful folks if it hadn't been for Mindy Farmer, the director of the May 4 Visitors Center at Kent State; Lori Boes, assistant director; and their student volunteers. All I had to do was mention a dilemma and they were on it, showering me with resources and their warm smiles. So smart, and so willing to help. "Anything you need, Debbie, we're here for you."

They are there for you, too. Any storyteller worth her salt tries to "go there," if possible, for when you go there, you, too, become part of the story, part of the continuum, part of the living memory of a place. So let's go there:

The May 4 Visitors Center on the Kent State campus is the place to begin your pilgrimage. It is a museum filled with important visual and audio context as well as exhibits on every facet of the late sixties, the Vietnam War and anti-war protests, and the events that transpired at Kent State and the aftermath. It is your number one must-visit destination, as it is situated in Taylor Hall at the top of Blanket Hill, overlooking the Commons and the Victory Bell on one side and the parking lot where the shootings occurred on the other.

The best way to get a feel for the tragedy of May 4, and to understand your place in its legacy, is to visit. Let Mindy and Lori know you are coming, and they will be ready for you. Come on the May 4 weekend, and you can take part in the vigil. It will change you.

In my research efforts, Mindy and Lori led me to professor emeritus Jerry Lewis, who wore a faculty marshal armband on that May weekend, and whose memories were naturally from a different—and important—perspective. We spoke by phone about that weekend, and I read his good book, *Kent State and May 4: A Social Science Perspective*, in manuscript form in the May 4 Collection at the Special Collections and Archives, in the Kent State University Library.

The May 4 Collection is your second must-visit destination on the Kent State campus. It is a treasure trove—literally a treasure trove, as archives are meant to be—of primary source material about the Kent State shootings. Letters, newspapers, flyers, campus arrest reports, police reports, photographs (so many photographs), position papers, dissertations, speeches, books, magazines, minutes of meetings, including clubs and organizations such as SDS (Students for a Democratic Society) and BUS (Black United Students), and much, much more.

I spent three days thoroughly enmeshed in boxes full of primary source material with the help of archivist Lae'l Hughes-Watkins and an assist from associate professor and former faculty advisor to the May 4 Task Force, Idris Kabir Syed.

Much of this May 4 material is digitized, and you can see it online here:

https://www.library.kent.edu/special-collections-and-archives /kent-state-shootings-may-4-collection. The May 4 Collection online is perhaps the best place to start your search for more about what most on campus call simply "May 4." Then you can plan your trip.

A tragedy like this one splits a town (not to mention a country) apart, and Kent is no exception. For years, the "town and gown" sandpapery feelings between Kent and the college were similar to "the exuberant youth vs the establishment rules" rub of most small college towns. There were anti-war protests on other college campuses (before and) after Nixon's speech on the Cambodia incursion/ invasion, but there is no doubt that matters escalated quickly and got out of control at Kent State.

What helped me most in telling the "townie" stories of Kent State, and the National Guard stories, were the oral histories that have been collected and archived at the May 4 Collection as well as at the Kent Historical Society, the Kent Public Library, and the Ohio Historical Society. Many of these oral histories are also available online, and many are recorded, thanks to a number of volunteers, and especially Sandra Perlman Halem, a "townie" originally from Philadelphia, whose husband came to Kent State to teach in the art department in 1969.

Sandy founded the May 4th Oral History project in 1990 to ensure that as many personal stories as possible could be shared. She is a playwright and past president of the Kent Historical Society. She connected me with so many stories from townspeople who each had vital lives in Kent, from children to teens to business owners to senior citizens, all archived stories, all waiting for me to listen to them. She also interviewed some National Guard soldiers who were on campus at Kent State during the weekend of May 4, including one in particular, an anonymous guardsman whose story broke my heart.

These oral histories were my gold. This is why I always say when talking with students (with anyone), "Tell your story." You never know who may need it someday. I believe this is why we write as well. We write for faceless, nameless readers, perhaps many years from now, who may need our story. We write to find like souls to share the road with, and we write to remind ourselves that we were here. I needed those stories, and there they were.

I also needed Angela Johnson's stories of her African-American family in Kent on May 4. Black children were taught to assume there were always real bullets in a white officer's gun. This teaching was borne out eleven days after the Kent State murders when, at the historically black college Jackson State, in Mississippi, a group of protesting students was confronted by city and state police, who opened fire and killed Phillip Lafayette Gibbs and James Earl Green (a high school student), a tragedy that got little press coverage but that is chronicled every year at the May 4 observance. Black students at Kent State were told by their peers at BUS to stay away from the Commons on May 4, and most complied.

I discovered Black United Students in the May 4 archive. BUS was very politically active at Kent State in the late sixties and early seventies, changing the landscape and demographic of the college, as well as the academic programs there. The oral histories from BUS students became instrumental to understanding the landscape of and context for the collective memory of May 4 and its connection to today's history.

The most important thing, though, that both Angela and Sandra did for me was give me the courage to tell stories that weren't the mainstream stories in the press, that weren't the established "this is what happened" stories. Their encouragement gave me a way to honor the memories of those who were there but outside the main story.

Also outside the main story but very much a part of it was the Top 40 playlist of rock and roll in the late sixties and early seventies, especially protest songs, which fueled the disenchantment, disgust, and determination to resist of a young generation expected to embrace and sacrifice themselves for the U.S. war effort in Southeast Asia.

"War" was written by Norman Whitfield and Barrett Strong in 1969. It was originally recorded by the Temptations, but Motown worried about releasing a song full of rageful social commentary about the Vietnam War to the band's conservative fan base, so Edwin Starr sang it, and the song shot to the top of the Billboard Top 100, with a generation of young people screaming *absolutely nothing!* in answer to Starr's angry challenge, asking what war was good for.

Phil Ochs's fiery, furious energy fueled many a protest song he wrote and sang at countless anti-war rallies in the 1960s and 1970s, including "I Ain't Marchin' Anymore," a song with so much context about wars through the ages, and those they affected, it's worth a listen to hear what college students and other young people—like me—heard on their record turntables in the sixties, and what propelled our sensibilities about war.

Likewise, "Country Joe" McDonald was a prolific songwriter (still is, as of this 2019 writing) and penned the sarcastic ("Whoopie! We're all gonna die!") anti-war song "I Feel-Like-I'm-Fixin'-to-Die Rag" in 1965. He sang it at Woodstock in 1969, where he changed the cheer for his band, Fish, to another F-word and stirred the crowd of 400,000 into a frenzied war-hating (but peaceful!) machine. Country Joe put the blame for the war squarely on politicians and those who stood to benefit from it, just as Phil Ochs and many others did—exercising their First Amendment rights.

Meanwhile, Marvin Gaye had been receiving devastating letters from his brother, Frankie, who was doing a tour of duty in Vietnam. Those letters, combined with the news—"Have you read about those kids who were killed at Kent State?" he asked his Motown managers when they called to ask how the next album was coming along—culminated in 1971's *What's Going On?* The album chronicles Gaye's complete change of heart about how he wanted his music to sound and feel, and what he wanted to say next—which included the title single full of soul, telling mothers there were too many of them crying, and brothers, "there's far too many of you dying."

"Eve of Destruction" was written by nineteen-year-old songwriter P. F. Sloan and recorded by Barry McGuire, in one take, in 1965. McGuire's gruff, insistent voice and Sloan's lyrics—which included the Cold War; injustices in Selma, Alabama; and the assassination of President John F. Kennedy—catapulted the song to instant-hit status with young people, even though the critics initially labeled it "everything that is wrong with the youth culture." It became a mantra of the Vietnam War–era protest songs, young people accusing the establishment of denying the realities of war and insisting we were not on the eve of destruction.

"Ohio," sung by Crosby, Stills, Nash & Young, was written by Neil Young shortly after the Kent State shootings. Young later wrote, "It's still hard to believe I had to write this song."

These songs and so many like them helped change the national conversation about the war in Vietnam. The murders at Kent State happened on a world stage at the apex of that war. The deaths of Sandy Scheuer, Bill Schroeder, Jeff Miller, and Allison Krause, and the wounding of nine of their fellow students—one paralyzed permanently—brought the war home to American soil, galvanized a nation sick at heart of war—"How could this happen in America?"— and hastened the end of the war in Southeast Asia.

For more about the aftermath of the Kent State shootings, you can visit the May 4 Visitors Center or research online, where there is a monumental amount of material to sift through. You'll find contradictory facts and opinions, which will invite you to think for yourself and dig deeper, as I had to do.

You will uncover myths and mysteries, and faulty memories and cover-ups and even lies, as you put the story in context. Which perhaps will make you think:

What might have happened if President Lyndon Johnson hadn't lied about the Gulf of Tonkin attack in 1964, which catapulted the U.S. into war? What might have happened if Nixon had not invaded Cambodia; if Secretary of Defense Robert McNamara hadn't escalated the war, even when he knew it was unwinnable? (See the Pentagon Papers.) What would have happened if those in positions of power had listened to Walter Cronkite when he stopped reporting what his government told him to report and declared—on national television at the end of a CBS newscast in 1968—that the Vietnam War was unwinnable?

What would have happened if we had not, as a nation, dearly loved our myths and the biased and distorted misinformation from powerful vested interests, and had instead investigated the facts ourselves, found alternate news sources, and listened to the young whose lives were on the line every day?

And further—just as important—what would have happened if the Kent State students' First Amendment rights had been acknowledged and respected?

What might have happened? We have no answers for that. We have only this moment, now. We can make decisions to be informed as citizens, not accepting what we hear or see or read until we've dug deeper on our own, for context, for truth. We can listen. We can share. We can make commitments to the tenets of democracy that say we have freedom of speech, press, assembly, and petition in our public places.

This is not an easy task. But in a democracy, it is what is required. It is what is asked of us, and especially of young people. You.

To make our country a land of the free, we must resolutely be a home of the brave.

I want to thank my brave editor, David Levithan, at Scholastic, and the entire Scholastic team who believed in the importance of this book and gave it reach. Thanks especially to Elizabeth Parisi for her elegant design. I thank my agent, Steven Malk, whose enthusiasms for my work encourage me to be brave, and I thank my friends and family, who surrounded me with strongholds of love and care while I wrote this story. I include Julia and Tom Euclide, who gave me a home in Kent while I researched, and Jim Pearce, who is always home, no matter where I wander, or what story I tell.